THANKSGIVING With ME

by MARGARET WILLEY

illustrated by LLOYD BLOOM

A LAURA GERINGER BOOK

An Imprint of HarperCollinsPublishers

Thanksgiving With Me Text copyright © 1998 by Margaret Willey Illustrations copyright © 1998 by Lloyd Bloom Printed in the U.S.A. All rights reserved. http://www.harperchildrens.com
Library of Congress Cataloging-in-Publication Data Willey, Margaret.   Thanksgiving with me / by Margaret Willey ; illustrated by Lloyd Bloom.   p.   cm.   Summary: As a young girl
waits for her six uncles to arrive for Thanksgiving, she asks her mother to describe life with these brothers on past Thanksgivings.   ISBN 0-06-027113-2   [1. Uncles—Fiction.   2. Thanksgiving
Day—Fiction.   3. Stories in rhyme.]   I. Bloom, Lloyd, ill.   II. Title.   PZ8.3.W6692Th 1997   95-43627   [E]—dc20   CIP   AC   Typography by Christine Kettner
1 2 3 4 5 6 7 8 9 10   ❖   First Edition

Sit down, Mother, and tell me again.
When are my uncles coming? When?

All of your uncles will be here soon;
they promised to be here by afternoon.

We can watch for them at my windowsill—
Cory, Fred, Davey, Joe, Henry, and Will!

Tell me again of your house by the sea, and brothers a hundred times bigger than me!

Well, Cory sang louder than morning crows,
and Fred, he couldn't see past his nose.

Davey, the smallest, was strong as an ox,
and Joe stood ten feet tall in his socks.

Henry warbled until he was fed,

and Will's red hair stood
up straight on his head.

Sing me that
Thanksgiving song
you'd sing—

"Come in from the sea
and pull up your chairs,
join hands together
and say your prayers,

"then eat like wolves and lions and bears,

with your heads
to the ceiling and
your feet downstairs!"

*Again we'll call them
in from the sea—
again they'll have
Thanksgiving with me!*

I'll help you, Mother.
We'll cook a feast!

A tower of biscuits, a bushel of peas,
a tub of potatoes, a wheel of cheese,
a dozen pies, a barrel of juice,
cranberries, plums,
and a Thanksgiving goose!

Oh, the kitchen will quake,
the oven will roar,
the music will flow
from window and door!

The dancing will lift the planks from the floor.

Guitar and banjo and violin,
and Papa will play his mandolin.
You can ask them to play your favorite song—

"Little Birdy"—I'll sing along.

Oh, sometimes when I'm alone in my bed
I see all those uncles inside my head,
and I wish I could call them in from the sea
and they would be here in my room with me.

I miss them, Mother. Do you miss them, too?
Do you miss those brothers
who lived with you?

Oh, Mother, look there . . .

. . . coming 'round the hill,

with his hair sticking up—it's Uncle Will!

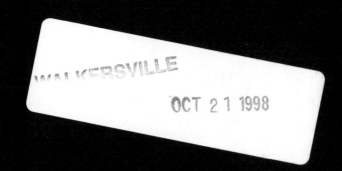